REVENGE OF THE ATOMIC BURPS

GARETH P. JONES

ILLUSTRATED BY

STEVE MAY

stripes

PET DEFENDERS

Protecting those who protect us

Did you know that Earth is under constant alien attack?

Don't worry.

We are the Pet Defenders, a secret society of domestic animals. We are your dogs, cats, rabbits and rodents. While you are off at school or work or doing whatever it is you humans do, we are keeping the Earth safe.

We keep our work hidden because we know what humans are like. The first sight of a Snot Snatcher or a Juggle-throated Bull Sniffler and you'll panic.

For Max, creator of Caboodle!
-GPJ

To Ann May, for innumerable good reasons
-SM

STRIPES PUBLISHING
An imprint of the Little Tiger Group
1 Coda Studios, 189 Munster Road,
London SW6 6AW

A paperback original
First published in Great Britain in 2018

Text copyright © Gareth P. Jones, 2018
Illustrations copyright © Steve May, 2018

ISBN: 978-1-84715-910-6

The right of Gareth P. Jones and Steve May to
be identified as the author and illustrator of this work
respectively has been asserted by them in accordance
with the Copyright, Designs and Patents Act, 1988.

Printed and bound in the UK.

10 9 8 7 6 5 4 3 2 1

Before you know it, you'll have blown up the very planet we're trying to defend.

Just carry on as normal — stroke your cats, take your dogs for walks and clean out your hamster cages. Don't forget to feed us, but please … let *us* take care of the aliens.

Now that you know all this, we need you to forget it. Our specially trained seagulls will take care of that. Ah, here they are with the Forget-Me-Plop now…

SSSPLAT!

CHAPTER 1

·:·

MRS STROGANOV'S DOG HOTEL

Biskit was having a bad day. It had started when he was suspended from his job as a Pet Defenders agent for encouraging a race of long-nosed aliens to secretly film the agency's activities. Biskit had his reasons for doing this but his grumpy rabbit boss, Commander F, hadn't wanted to hear them.

Trying to look on the bright side, Biskit thought he could spend some quality time with Philip.

But when he had returned to the flat, his owner was standing in the hallway with a suitcase.

"There you are, boy," said Philip. "Look, Biskit, I'm really sorry. If I could take you to Spain with me, I would. You'll be much better off in the kennels. It's only for a week."

Biskit's tail dropped between his legs and he bowed his head. He had forgotten that Philip had booked a holiday and was sending him to spend the whole week in Mrs Stroganov's Dog Hotel.

On the drive across town, Philip explained that Mrs Stroganov came highly recommended but all Biskit cared about was whether there was an escape route. Even though Biskit had been suspended, secret agents tasked with protecting Earth from alien invasions were no use to anyone if they were stuck in a back yard.

Philip parked outside a grey building and led Biskit to the door, where a short stern-faced woman with dark hair met them.

"Your dog will be well looked after here.

We keep all our dogs well fed, well walked and well contained." Mrs Stroganov looked pointedly at Biskit as she said this.

"Biskit's very important to me," said Philip. "He's basically family."

"You have no need to worry," said Mrs Stroganov. "We never have complaints. Our kennels have everything a dog needs and the back yard is secure."

"Oh, Biskit usually sleeps indoors," said Philip. "He's an apartment dog."

MRS STROGANOV'S DOG HOTEL

"Dogs need fresh air," Mrs Stroganov replied. "Let me show you the yard."

There were six kennels out the back. In one a grey-haired dachshund lay, fast asleep. A small yappy terrier ran out of another.

"Hi, hello, hey," barked the terrier. "My name's Jakey. I'm called Jakey. They call me Jakey. What's your name? What are you called? What do they call you?"

"Quiet your yapping," said Mrs Stroganov sternly.

"Sorry. Sorry. Sorry," said Jakey, before whispering to Biskit, "she doesn't like the yapping."

"You surprise me," replied Biskit. Being able to understand what Jakey was saying didn't make him any less annoying.

"This is Biskit's kennel," said Mrs Stroganov. "As you can see, we only have two other guests at present – Jakey and Old Mo."

Philip crouched down to talk to Biskit. "It seems OK, right?" he said, tickling his ears. "You'll hardly miss me at all."

Biskit didn't want to make Philip feel guilty – he deserved a holiday. Lately all he seemed to do was work, eat and sleep. Biskit licked Philip's hand and sat down.

Jakey ran around him in circles, barking excitedly. "How long are you here for? How long will you be here? How many days will you stay?"

"A week," replied Biskit.

"You see, the dogs are already getting on," said Mrs Stroganov. "It's almost as though they can understand each other." She laughed at the idea. "Now, we run a tight ship here. Mealtimes are at ten o'clock, two o'clock and five o'clock, followed by a brisk walk. Leads will be kept on at all times. There will be no funny business."

"Oh, Biskit's a good dog," said Philip. "You won't have any trouble."

"I hope not. Trouble will not be tolerated," said Mrs Stroganov.

"Well then, boy, I guess this is it," said Philip.

He ruffled Biskit's fur, then went back inside with Mrs Stroganov. Biskit watched the door slam shut and let out a groan.

"New inmate, eh?" said a voice from the other kennel.

Biskit turned to see the dachshund standing up.

"Hey, Old Mo," said Jakey. "Look! We've got a

new pal. We're going to have a ball. I love balls. Do you like balls? Or do you prefer sticks?"

"This one can be a bit annoying," said Old Mo with a heavy sigh, "but meals and walks are regular. When you get to my age you appreciate the routine."

"Don't I recognize you?" said Biskit. "Wait a minute – you're Agent Mo. You're a Pet Defenders agent."

Old Mo shook his head. "*Used* to be. My defending days are behind me."

"I remember you giving a talk when I was a new recruit. You taught me my most valuable lesson: a good agent always trusts his nose," said Biskit.

Old Mo smiled sadly. "Yeah, well, I lost my sense of smell years ago," he said. "I remember you, now I think about it. You were an annoying little upstart. Didn't you partner up with Champ?"

"Yes," said Biskit, feeling a tinge of sadness at the mention of his former partner.

"Now, there was a promising agent," said Old Mo.

"He fell into a portal and ended up on the other side of the galaxy," said Biskit. "He hasn't been seen since."

"Shame. So, you're on your own now, are you?"

"No, I have a new partner – Mitzy. She's a cat."

"A cat," barked Jakey. "Where? Where's the cat?"

Old Mo ignored him. "Dogs and cats, working together. Things have changed since my day. I guess it's for the better. How's the bunny?"

"Commander F suspended me this morning," said Biskit.

Old Mo smiled. "Oh well, it's not as though you're getting out of here any time soon. The walls are two metres high. Sorry, Biskit, you're here until your owner comes to collect you."

"They haven't built the kennel that can contain me yet," bragged Biskit.

"Yes, that's how I remember you," said Old Mo. "Overconfident and reckless. Now if you don't mind, I was in the middle of a rather good dream about rabbits. Wake me up at ten, would you? Jakey, try to keep the noise down."

"I won't make any noise. Oh, look, a pigeon. Up there on the wall, a pigeon," he yapped. "Let's bark at the pigeon. I love barking."

Biskit flopped his ears over his eyes. It was going to be a long week.

CHAPTER 2

SECOND FIRST ENCOUNTER

Mitzy had tried to persuade Commander F to reconsider Biskit's suspension but the cat's words had fallen on deaf ears.

"That dog needs to learn who's in charge of this operation," said the large white rabbit, chewing a stick of celery. "He has to follow the rules rather than trusting his instincts."

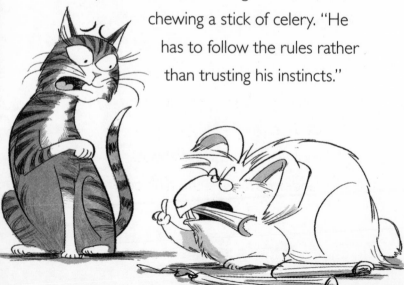

"Biskit's instincts are what make him such a good agent," said Mitzy. "We need him."

"And I need you to stop arguing with your superior," snarled Commander F. "We've had a report of alien activity at one of the factories on the outskirts of town."

"What kind of alien activity?" asked Mitzy.

"I don't have any details. Our entire seagull network is down. Example One says it's some kind of technical glitch."

Usually the Pet Defenders kept in contact via a network of trained seagulls. These birds wore cameras, voice communicators, medical kits and packages of Forget-Me-Plop.

"Every seagull is grounded until the system is up and running again," said Commander F, "so I won't be able to keep an eye on you."

"I'll be fine," said Mitzy.

"It's not you I'm worried about."

Commander F waggled the nibbled end of

the celery stick at her. "Our ability to wipe witnesses' memories is the most important tool we have to keep our operation secret."

"I won't let you down, sir."

Mitzy wished she felt as confident as she sounded. She left Commander F to finish off his celery and made her way across town.

When she reached the cluster of factories, she jumped up and over a wall into the car park. She approached cautiously, using the vans and lorries for cover.

"Psst. Over here. Are you the Pet Defenders agent?"

Hearing the voice, Mitzy turned to see a grey rat tucked between two wheels of a lorry.

"Crisp?" She recognized him as the street rat who had recently been abducted by a Snot Snatcher.

"How do you know my name?" he replied.

When the seagull had made Crisp forget his alien abduction, it had also removed all memory of meeting Mitzy.

"It's my job to know stuff. I'm Agent Mitzy," she replied. "Did you report some unusual activity?"

"Yes. I was here scavenging. There's usually good grub in those bins around the side. That building over there is a fish-finger factory. Sometimes you can pick up these great big bags of breadcrumbs… Delicious! And the one on that side makes frozen pizzas. Really nice toppings—"

"Crisp," interrupted Mitzy.

"Oh, it's all right for you domestic animals with your food bowls," said Crisp bitterly.

"I'm a street cat," said Mitzy. "Get to the unusual bit."

"Oh, right. Sorry. I saw something walk into that building." Crisp pointed his nose at the door of a nearby factory. His voice trembled with fear. "I've … I've never seen anything like it. I don't think it was from this planet."

"Can you describe it?" asked Mitzy.

"It's made of bricks and it has huge chimneys sticking out of the top," said Crisp.

"I meant the alien, not the building," said Mitzy with a sigh.

"Oh, that. Yes, it was big, green and spiky with eyes on stalks."

The lorry revved its engine. Mitzy and Crisp moved quickly to another lorry, with an advert for a fizzy drink on its side. Curly straws spelt out the words:

"Then what happened?" asked Mitzy.

Sip Pop
TO FEEL
Tip Top!

"A black cat followed it in."

"A black cat?" said Mitzy.

"Yes, but it had space gadgets! It wore a flashing collar and had a pointy gun thing on its tail. It looked pretty cool actually."

"OK, I'll take it from here. You can get back to scavenging."

Mitzy snuck out from under the fizzy drinks lorry.

"Get back to scavenging? After this?" said Crisp, joining her. "It's the most amazing thing that's ever happened to me."

CHAPTER 3

❧

UNSMASHED WINDOW

According to Pet Defenders guidelines, Mitzy wasn't allowed to tell Crisp about his previous alien encounter. The rules also advised against letting witnesses become too involved in cases.

"Crisp, please go about your business and let me go about mine," said Mitzy.

"No way. This is far too much fun," said Crisp, following her. "I'm sticking with you like chewing gum. Come on, I'll show you where they went."

Crisp scurried towards the factory.

"Wait," said Mitzy. "Someone's coming out."

The door slid open. Mitzy darted forwards, snatched Crisp in her mouth and dived for the cover of a nearby car. A young male factory worker with long greasy hair stepped out and limped towards the fizzy drinks lorry.

"Now's our chance," said Crisp. "While the door's open." He wriggled free and ran forwards. Mitzy had no choice but to follow him into the reception area. Inside, everything was branded with the same logo as the lorry and the walls were lined with framed adverts with various slogans:

Sip PoP
ENERGY POWER!
Down a can every hour

Sip PoP
LEMON & LIME
Drink one now while there is still time

Sip PoP
RASPERRY RED
In a glass, a bottle or in bed

A receptionist was sitting behind the desk, reading a book. The phone was ringing but she was too engrossed in her book to answer it.

"Stay close," urged Mitzy, ducking behind an enormous plastic bottle of pop.

"Oh look, Sip Pop Cherry," said Crisp, joining her. "It's great to drink when you feel merry."

"Keep quiet." Mitzy poked her head around the side of the bottle. The receptionist was still staring at her book. "Come on."

Mitzy and Crisp made a dash for the corridor but they stopped as soon as they turned the corner. A female factory worker was standing right in front of them.

"What do we do?" whispered Crisp.

"Let's see what she does," replied Mitzy.

But the woman didn't do anything. She was standing still, staring at nothing. She wasn't even blinking.

"What's wrong with her?" asked Crisp.

Mitzy turned around to look at the receptionist, who was also perfectly still.

"It looks like they've all got the Stares," said Mitzy.

"But this is the ground floor," said Crisp.

"*Stares* not stairs," said Mitzy. "It stands for a State of Time and Reality Experience Suspension. I've seen Barb do it on people."

"Who's Barb?"

"An alien fish," said Mitzy, "but she's on our side – unlike whoever did this."

"So it's like a freeze ray?" said Crisp.

"Yes." Mitzy slipped past the woman and peered into one of the rooms off the corridor. There were two more unmoving factory workers. One was holding a heavy-looking cardboard box. The other was bending down to pick up a crate of bottles. Mitzy moved on to the next door, where there were more static humans.

"Why would anyone want to do this to a fizzy drinks factory?" she mused.

"Maybe we could ask him," said Crisp.

Mitzy turned. At the other end of the corridor, standing on a windowsill, was a cat.

He looked at them. Just as Crisp had described, he had jet-black fur and was wearing a collar covered in small flashing lights. He also had a ray gun attached to his tail.

"Stop right there," said Crisp. "We're the Pet Defenders."

"Crisp, please leave the talking to me," said Mitzy.

"Sorry," said Crisp.

She turned to address the cat. "Welcome to Planet Earth. I'm Agent Mitzy of the Pet Defenders and it's my job to defend this planet. If you come in peace, I ask that you leave in peace."

The black cat smiled. "Listen, small worlder, there's a big universe out there and I've got a job to do. Please don't get in my way."

"What did you call me?"

"A small worlder. Protecting your little planet with no understanding of what's actually going on in the rest of your galaxy."

"What's all that stuff you're wearing?" asked Crisp, captivated by the coloured lights that were flashing on the cat's collar, always in the same order: red, blue, green, yellow then purple.

The cat gave him a snooty look. "It's a standard issue SUPA Ray Blaster. The collar operates the tail gun, allowing me to select from one of five settings. Look, I'll show you the Stare Ray."

The black cat swung his tail gun then nudged the blue button with his chin, firing a laser beam directly at Crisp and freezing him to the spot.

"Crisp," said Mitzy.

The rat stared blankly ahead.

Mitzy turned back to the cat. "You can't do that! This is my planet."

"Spoken like a true small worlder."

"Stop calling me that. Who are you?" demanded Mitzy.

"The name is Zed," said the black cat. "But I'm rather busy right now so I'm afraid I can't stop and chat."

He swung his tail around, aimed it at the window then pushed the red button. A laser beam shot from the gun and shattered the glass. Zed hopped through the hole and turned back to look at Mitzy. "Stay out of my way, Agent Mitzy."

"Sorry, I can't do that." Mitzy jumped up on to

the windowsill
to follow Zed
but, as she did,
the black cat
pressed the
green button
on his collar. This
time the laser
beam hit the spot
where the window

had been. There was a flash of light, then the
tiny shards of glass from the broken window
leaped into the air and reassembled themselves
as if the window had never been broken.

By the time Mitzy realized what was
happening, her nose had already slammed
into the glass. She dropped down on to the
windowsill in a crumpled heap and watched as
the black cat strolled away.

"What happened?" asked Crisp, waking from

his stupor.

"I don't know." Mitzy waggled a paw, checking nothing was broken. "He smashed the window and then he…" She hesitated, unsure how to explain it. "… he unsmashed it."

"Unsmashed?" said Crisp. "Why don't I remember that?"

"He hit you with a Stare Ray."

"How come it wore off so quickly?" said Crisp, looking at the humans who were still frozen.

"I don't know, but I know a mouse who will know. We'll check the area, then go and see Example One."

"But what about the other alien I saw enter the factory, the one with the spikes?" asked Crisp.

"I have a feeling that whatever that thing was, it's gone," said Mitzy.

"How do you know that?"

"I don't. It's more of an instinct," she replied.

CHAPTER 4

CHAMP'S RETURN

Biskit was bored. There was nothing to do at Mrs Stroganov's Dog Hotel except stare at the walls while listening to Old Mo snore and Jakey yap constantly. He occupied his mind by working out possible escape plans. Old Mo had been right when he said that the walls were too high to jump. The only way out would be through the building. Biskit had observed how Mrs Stroganov always pushed open the door with her elbows when she was carrying refills for the food bowls, then left it to swing shut behind her. It took three seconds to close.

There was room to get past her but the problem was how to get through the front door in time as well.

"Jakey," he said. "I've got an idea—"

"An idea! Brilliant," he barked. "That sounds great. I love ideas."

"Yes, but I'll need you to concentrate."

"Oh, I love concentrating. I'm great at concentrating. Hey, what's that?"

Biskit sighed. This wasn't going to be easy. "Jakey," he said. "Listen to me…"

But Jakey was staring at the top of the wall. Biskit turned to look. Two white paws had appeared.

"Someone's climbing in," barked Jakey.

"That's a big jump to get up there," said Biskit.

"The other side isn't as high," said Jakey. "She's not as worried about dogs trying to get into this place."

"If it is a dog…" Biskit watched as a black and white shaggy head appeared. It was a dog all right but it wasn't any old dog. It was an Old English sheepdog that Biskit knew extremely well.

"Champ?" he said. "Is it really you?"

The sheepdog landed inside the yard with surprising ease and looked at Biskit.

"Biskit," said Champ. "Good to see you."

Biskit caught a whiff of an unusual scent. He eyed Champ cautiously.

"I know what you're going to say," said Champ. "You're going to tell me I smell different. Well, a lot has changed since I last saw you. Besides, I'd like to see how you would smell after flying halfway across the universe in a cat-litter tray."

"A litter tray?" repeated Biskit.

"Yes, my partner's. He's called Zed. He's a good agent but I wish he'd lay off the spicy food." Champ pulled a face.

"What partner?" said Biskit. "What are you talking about?"

"Oh good. You're confused, too," said Jakey. "I'm really confused."

"Then maybe stay quiet, Jakey," growled Biskit.

Old Mo stepped out of his kennel. "Well I never. Champ! Biskit said you'd gone missing."

To Biskit's surprise, Champ snarled at the old dachshund, showing his teeth.

"Champ?" said Biskit. "It's Agent Mo. We used to look up to him back when we were rookie agents. Remember?"

For a sheepdog, Champ looked decidedly sheepish. "Oh yes, sorry," he said. "It's good to see you."

"Hey. I'm Jakey," yapped the little dog. "My name is Jakey. You can call me Jakey."

Biskit silenced him with a look. "Champ, you need to explain what you're doing here. You're acting very strangely."

"Biskit, can we talk about this on the way?" said Champ.

"On the way where?" asked Biskit.

"To catch the bad guys, of course. That's why I'm here. I need your help to track an alien. Now, how do we get out of here?"

Biskit couldn't help smiling. His partner was back and he needed his help. Biskit turned to Jakey. "OK, Jakey, Champ and I are going to escape. I need you to bark as loudly as you can."

"I can do that," said Jakey. "What should I bark about? Pigeons? Planes? Barking? I don't mind. I just love barking. I love it. **Bark, bark, bark**, that's me."

While Jakey barked at the top of his voice about what he should be barking about, Biskit said quietly to Old Mo, "I'll need someone to keep Mrs Stroganov busy while we get out."

"Leave it to me," said Old Mo. "Champ, it was good to see you again."

"You, too, Old No."

"Old *Mo*," said Biskit.

Bark!

Bark!

Bark!

Bark!

Bark!

Bar

Bar

Bark!

Bar

"That's what I meant," said Champ. "Come on, we need to move fast."

At that moment Mrs Stroganov opened the door. "Quieten down," she shouted. "None of your yapping! Stop barking!"

Old Mo charged at Mrs Stroganov, making her spin around. Biskit took the chance to run past her with Champ close behind. They were at the front door in seconds. Biskit jumped up and grabbed the handle with his mouth while

Champ barged at the door. It swung open and they darted through.

As soon as they were out of the house, Biskit and Champ jumped over a low fence and ducked down behind a bush. They heard the door open again and Mrs Stroganov's voice saying, "Bad dog. Where are you? And your friend? You get back here now. You must return at once! Your owner will not be happy."

They waited until she had set off down the street, looking for them, before they headed off in the other direction, moving quickly through the back streets.

"Where are we going?" asked Biskit.

"The ship," said Champ. "Come on."

"What ship? Where have you been all this time?"

"A lot of places. I was recruited by the Special Universal Policing Agency. I'm a SUPA agent now. It's like the Pet Defenders only on a much bigger scale."

"The what?" said Biskit.

"I'll explain back at the ship."

"You've got a ship?"

"No, it's Zed's ship. Come on."

CHAPTER 5

🐾

NERD ALERT

Mitzy and Crisp could find no sign of the spiky alien or the black cat around the fizzy drinks factory. The effects of the Stare Ray were beginning to wear off the factory workers, so Mitzy told Crisp it was time for them to go.

"Won't they wonder what happened?" asked Crisp.

"We'll wipe their memories once our seagull network is back up. I'm sure Example One will have it working again soon," said Mitzy. "Come on."

On the way to the NERD lab, Mitzy wished more than ever that Biskit was with her. He would easily be able to sniff out the mysterious black cat. But instead of a dog that could smell well, she was stuck with a rat that smelled awful for company. Still, she liked having someone to talk to … even if she did have to explain everything twice.

"Is Example One a cat, too?" Crisp asked as they crossed the patch of wasteland on the outskirts of town.

"He's a mouse. He was a lab mouse until he was injected with a brain-growing formula. Ever since, he has been the Pet Defenders' best scientist. He's probably the most intelligent animal on the planet."

"No, that's my uncle Falafel. He invented the Everything Sandwich. What you do is you put everything you find between two pieces of bread and eat it. Genius."

They reached an old boarded-up door around the back of the lab. "Crisp, maybe you should leave the talking to me this time."

Mitzy pushed aside one of the boards that blocked the door and entered a brightly lit room. Crisp scampered in behind her then stopped to looked around in wonder. There were mice clutching clipboards, observing test tubes overflowing with glowing goo. The shelves were filled with glass jars containing swimming beards and mysterious alien dung. Mitzy led Crisp to a room in which a pink mouse with glasses was dancing in front of a mirror. Electronic music was playing loudly while the mouse leaped, shimmied and moonwalked.

"Busy then?" said Mitzy.

Example One turned a slightly redder tinge of pink than usual and hurriedly turned down the music on his miniature tablet. "Yes, actually, I am very busy. I'm trying to get the communications back up again."

"By dancing in front of a mirror?"

"Some of my passwords are dance-coded. I have to perform a certain number of moves to get into the system." Example One held up the tablet. A blue box appeared with the words:

> ## PASSWORD CORRECT.
> ## SYSTEM OPEN.

"Does that make it more secure?" asked Mitzy.

"Yes and it's also an excellent way to keep fit. So, who's the rat? A new recruit?" asked Example One.

"No, he's... He's not important."

"Thanks," said Crisp.

"I didn't mean it like that." She turned to Example One. "There's an ongoing alien threat. I need the seagulls back in the air. We have a factory full of potential witnesses and at least two suspected aliens on the loose."

Example One took off his glasses and cleaned them with a small cloth. "I'm working on it but something is blocking the system. It could be the very aliens you're trying to find. Whoever is doing it, they must be very advanced to hack my system. Or possibly they're just a very good dancer."

"I ran into a cat packing some serious space tech earlier," said Mitzy.

Example One picked up his tablet and a stylus. "What kind of thing?" he asked, poised to jot down the details.

"It had five settings. The blue button gave people the Stares."

"Hmm, a Stare Ray," said Example One. "Common enough in many parts of the universe."

"Any idea why it had a longer-lasting effect on the humans than on Crisp?"

Example One tapped his stylus on his tablet. "I believe it's dependent on the brain size of the target," he said. "The larger the brain, the longer it lasts."

Mitzy laughed.

"What?" said Crisp. "What's funny?"

"Nothing." Mitzy turned back to Example One. "The red ray smashed the window."

"That's probably a standard Blast Ray," said Example One.

"Then there was the green one," added Mitzy. "That was really weird. It repaired the window."

"Repaired it?" asked Example One. "How

remarkable."

"It made everything go kind of weird, then it was like the window had never smashed."

"Ooh, now that sounds like an Unmistaker. I've heard about them but I've never seen one in action."

"Did you say an *Unmistaker*?" said Mitzy.

"Yes, it's a localized time-alteration device," said Example One. "It sends a set number of molecules back in time by a few seconds, so the damage is undone."

"Like a time machine?" said Crisp.

Example One looked at him. "Who are you again?" he asked.

"Never mind him," said Mitzy. "You were saying?"

"Yes, it's not *quite* a time machine. It doesn't send everything back in time – just its target. And only by a few seconds – a couple of minutes, at a stretch. An alien with technology like that would certainly be capable of blocking our signals."

"It wasn't an alien," said Crisp. "It was a cat."

"A common misunderstanding," said Example One. "There are billions of planets in the universe containing zillions of creatures. It's only natural that some have evolved to look the same as Earth animals. You didn't think all aliens were little green men with stalks on their heads, did you?"

"Ooh, I saw one of those today, too," said Crisp.

"Really?" said Example One.

"Yes. We're trying to track them both down," said Mitzy. "I mean, *I'm* trying to track them down."

"Without our communications system, I don't know how I can help," said Example One.

"I can," said Crisp.

"You?" said Mitzy. "How can you help?"

"I've got cousins all over this town. If I put the word out, we'll find this cat in no time."

"Given the circumstances, that might be your best option," said Example One.

"OK, Crisp, let's give it a go," said Mitzy.

"Hey, rats trying to catch a cat," said Crisp. "That's funny, right?"

"Hilarious," replied Mitzy.

CHAPTER 6

THE CABOODLE BROTHERS

Biskit followed Champ to one of Nothington-on-Sea's quieter parks. It felt strange to be running alongside his old partner again. After all this time, Champ was back. Biskit should have felt happy but he still had a nagging feeling that something was wrong.

There were a few humans in the park – jogging, sitting on benches or walking dogs – but Champ led Biskit to a quiet wooded area behind some tennis courts.

"Hold on. I just need to do something." Biskit sniffed a tree then cocked his hind leg up against it.

"Hey," said Champ. "Not there."

"Why?" asked Biskit, lowering his leg.

"I'll show you." Champ nudged his nose against a knot in the tree bark. The tree beeped then a door appeared, revealing the interior of a spaceship that was much bigger than the tree.

"This is your ship?" said Biskit. "A tree?"

"It's camouflaged," said Champ. "It blends in with its surroundings. All SUPA agents have one. Come on in. I'll show you around."

Biskit tried not to feel jealous as he followed Champ inside.

It wasn't the first spaceship he had been in but it was by far the slickest. It had rows of flashing buttons and screens showing readings. Every door slid silently open as he approached.

"What kind of ship is this?" asked Biskit.

"A molecular spectrum ship," said Champ. "Rather than travelling through space, it slips through spaces."

"Oh, right." Biskit was fine fighting aliens but he often struggled with the science stuff. "Who did you say it belonged to?"

"A cat called Zed," replied Champ. "He's my partner."

"Your new partner is a cat?" Biskit tried to hide the jealousy that bubbled up inside of him.

"Yes," said Champ.

"So why did you have to travel here in his kitty litter?" Biskit was desperately trying to keep up.

"I snuck on board. SUPA agents aren't

allowed to go back to their home planets. It's one of the rules. They're concerned it might compromise one of their agents. I mean, *our* agents. I'm one of them, obviously."

"So why have you come back now?"

"Let me show you."

Champ jumped on to a control panel and pressed a button. All of a sudden, a screen on the spaceship's wall revealed an image of a prison cell containing two strange creatures. One was blue, the other was green. They both had prickles all over their bodies, multicoloured feet and eyes on stalks.

"Who are they?" asked Biskit.

"Atomic Burps," said Champ. "These ones are brothers. Twist and Stick Caboodle."

"What's an Atomic Burp?"

"They're shapeshifters," said Champ. "Carbon-dioxide consumption causes a release of air from their stomach so powerful that it alters their appearance at an atomic level."

"Right..." Biskit nodded wisely.

"Fizzy drinks make them change shape. One burp is powerful enough to transform them into anything they want: a dog, a cat, a solar moth, a Bottopotamus of Bomping Flex ... anything."

"So why would they choose to look like that?" said Biskit with a chuckle.

The shadow of a frown passed over Champ's face but then he smiled and said, "I suppose they *are* weird-looking compared to us hairy quadrupeds, now you mention it."

"Why are they in prison?" asked Biskit.

"They're bank robbers. They were planning to rob the vaults of the Central Intergalactic Bank when I caught them. Unfortunately, they got out."

"They escaped?"

"Yes. Watch." On the screen, two drinks materialized inside the prison cell. Both of the Atomic Burps drank, then the alien with green skin let out a loud **buuurrrrpppp** and his body rippled and shimmered. His spikes curled in on themselves and he turned into a small flying creature with a pointy tail.

"Is that a Maybe Fly-Mite?" asked Biskit.

"It's a Might-Be Mayfly," said Champ.

The newly transformed alien flew through the bars, while the blue one placed his hands on his hips.

"So only one of the brothers got out," said Biskit.

"That was Stick who just escaped. It took Twist longer to build up enough burp power to get out but he was out by the following day."

"And you think they're on Earth? What would they be doing here?"

"Wouldn't you like to know!" said Champ. "I mean, wouldn't we *all* like to know! The important thing now is to catch them – and for that we need your nose."

"My nose?"

"Yes," said Champ. "I need you to help me sniff out these thieves and get them back behind bars where they belong."

"Just like old times," said Biskit.

"Exactly," replied Champ. "This ship can

supply you with the scent. Place your nose here."

Champ indicated a small horn that jutted out of the control panel. Biskit pushed his nose inside and Champ pressed a button. Biskit had smelled life forms from every corner of the universe and he never forgot a scent. This one was vinegary with a lingering whiff of mouldy onion.

"Atomic Burps have a totally unique scent," said Champ.

"It's not that unique," said Biskit. "It smells like you."

Champ scratched his nose with his paw and coughed. "I spent a week with these two in my ship when I arrested them. I'm not surprised their scent rubbed off on me. So? Are you ready to go track a Burp, partner?"

Hearing Champ call him *partner* after all

this time, Biskit couldn't help but smile.
"But Champ, these Atomic Burps could be
anywhere. I'm good but even I can't smell
something on the other side of town."

"You can if you use this." Champ picked up
what looked like a metal bracelet. "Stand still."
Champ spoke through his teeth as he placed
the bracelet over Biskit's nose.

"What is it?" asked Biskit.

"It's a SUPA Super Smeller. It amplifies your
sense of smell." Champ pressed a button that
opened the external door.

Biskit sniffed and felt a thousand scents drift
into his mind, informing him of every living
creature in the park. "Wow," he said. "Let's get
out and find these Burps."

Stepping out of the ship, a breeze
rustled through the tree's

branches and brought with it a collection of smells. Biskit could detect every animal in the area. He could even smell the honey on the leg of a passing bee.

But no Burp.

"Anything?" said Champ.

Biskit moved into a clearing and sniffed again. He could smell flowers, plants, a packet of biscuits being eaten by a toddler, a baby who needed a fresh nappy, a cup of coffee spilled in the dirt, an orange peel… He had to sniff further. He had to find the alien scent.

"I know you can do this," said Champ.

Biskit closed his eyes and inhaled again. He smelled the exhaust fumes of cars, a jogger sweating, a microwave meal being

cooked. There were so many smells, but he sifted through each one until he found the scent he was searching for. It was so faint he almost missed it. He turned his head to the left and the scent vanished altogether. He turned his head back and found it again. His feet hadn't moved but the SUPA Super Smeller allowed him to hone in on the Atomic Burp. Making a series of tiny movements with his head he was able to move towards it. Then he picked up the scent of something much nearer and much more familiar.

Biskit opened his eyes.

"What?" said Champ. "Have you got it?"

"Yes, I've got your alien robber. But there's someone I need to talk to first."

"Who?" asked Champ.

"My partner, Mitzy."

CHAPTER 7

‧‧‧

SUPA AGENT ZED

It didn't take long for Crisp to find another rat and pass on the word that they were looking for a black cat with a tin pot on his head.

"What happens now?" asked Mitzy as they headed back into town.

"That rat will tell the next rat he meets who will tell two more, then four more, then eight and so on. Rats can get a message across town in minutes."

Mitzy was doubtful it would work but, sure enough, by the time they reached the train station a dark grey rat called Burger scuttled out from a bush to inform Crisp that the "tin-pot black cat" had just been spotted entering a park on the east side of town. Mitzy was impressed.

When they reached the fence that surrounded the park, Crisp snuck under it while Mitzy found a hole to slip through. Mitzy could hear a baby crying as a toddler munched through a packet of biscuits and their mother chatted on a phone.

"What's that, love?" she was saying. "Luke is screaming his head off. No idea what's wrong with him. Oscar, give him a biscuit, would you? Oops."

Something cold and brown sprayed down as a paper coffee cup landed in front of Mitzy.

"Great. Now I've dropped my coffee," said the woman.

Mitzy darted out of the way. Crisp swerved to avoid her and skidded on a piece of orange peel.

"**RAAAAat!**" squealed the
toddler. "**Cat and raaaaat!**"

Mitzy and Crisp moved quickly, leaving the
family behind them. They were running round
the side of a tennis court when they found a
scruffy mongrel and an Old English sheepdog
blocking their path.

"Out of the way," said Crisp. "This is Pet
Defenders' business."

"I couldn't have put it better myself," said
Biskit, winking at Mitzy.

"Biskit meet Crisp!" said Mitzy. "Who's your
friend?"

"It's Champ," said Biskit.

"Champ?" said Mitzy. "As in your old
partner, Champ?"

"Who are you calling old?" asked Champ.

Mitzy and Biskit looked at one another in
silence. Mitzy hated how jealous she felt. She

wanted to protest that Biskit was her partner now. Instead, an awkward silence descended until another voice broke it.

"Nobody move."

Biskit, Champ, Mitzy and Crisp turned to see Zed jump down from a tree branch and prowl towards them, his tail gun swinging threateningly.

"What are you doing here, Champ?" said Zed.

"You two know each other?" said Biskit.

"Yes, we're both SUPA agents," replied Zed.

"You're what?" asked Mitzy.

"We work for the Special Universal Policing Agency," said Zed. "Now, would you mind telling me what you're doing here on your home planet, Champ? You know it's against agency rules."

"I'm the only agent ever to successfully arrest

the Caboodle Brothers," replied Champ.

"So why is this mongrel wearing my SUPA tech?" asked Zed, indicating the device on Biskit's nose.

"Zed, meet Biskit," said Champ.

"Biskit? As in your ex-partner, Biskit?" said Zed. "The one you go on about all the time?"

Biskit glanced at Champ, but he was staring intently at Zed.

"I am so confused," said Crisp. "So the two dogs used to be partners with each other but now they're both partners with the two cats, in which case how come—"

"Keep quiet, rat." Zed hit the blue button on his collar, firing a beam of light at Crisp. The rat froze.

"Stop zapping Crisp!" said Mitzy.

"You'll be next, if you're not careful," said Zed. "I'm here on important business. There are two Atomic Burps on the loose and I'm

going to bring them in."

"Yeah, right," growled Champ.

"What does that mean?" said Zed.

"It means I'll be the one who brings them in," said Champ.

"This bickering isn't helping," said Mitzy. "Now, what do these Burps look like?"

"We don't know," said Biskit. "They're shapeshifters. One burp and they could be anything."

"Exactly," said Champ, eyeing Mitzy. "Maybe *you're* one of them."

Mitzy felt her fur stand on end as Champ stared at her suspiciously and Zed pointed his tail gun at her head, his chin hovering over the red button.

"Lower your weapon," said Biskit. "That's my partner."

"Yes," said Mitzy. "And this is our planet to defend."

Zed smiled but kept his tail gun aimed at Mitzy as he moved in a circle around her. "Walk."

"What?"

"Walk. I hit that Burp's leg back at the factory," said Zed. "I want to see if you have a limp."

"I don't have a limp," said Mitzy, taking a few steps to prove it. "Hold on. I saw a man with a limp back at the factory. He got into a lorry of fizzy drinks."

"That sounds like Stick," said Zed. "Fizzy drinks are like rocket fuel to Atomic Burps."

"We'd be able to find him if our communications weren't down," said Mitzy.

"That's Zed's fault," said Champ. "He's jamming your entire system."

"He's right," said Zed. "It's standard procedure to block all small-worlder agency transmissions."

"Small worlder?" barked Biskit.

"We don't have time for all this," said Mitzy. "Zed, we need you to turn off the jamming device so we can locate this Atomic Burp."

"There's no need," said Champ. "The SUPA Super Smeller means that Biskit has the alien scent. He'll lead us to the aliens."

"You shouldn't even be here," said Zed.

"Yes, but I am here and we have a job to do," said Champ. "Biskit and I will go after Stick. You cats can go get the communications back up."

"No. I'm staying with my partner," said Mitzy pointedly.

Champ smiled. "Fine. In which case, Zed can go back to the ship while we deal with this criminal."

"Sounds like a plan," said Biskit.

Zed looked warily at them all. "OK, I'm putting my trust in you, Champ, because you're my partner, but keep an eye on these two."

"They'll be fine," said Champ. "Leave it to me."

Crisp blinked as the effect of the Stare Ray wore off. "Hey, what's going on? Did that cat shoot me with his—"

Zed fired the Stare Ray at Crisp again.

"What have you got against him?" asked Mitzy.

Zed shrugged. "What can I say? I don't like rats."

CHAPTER 8

•••

TROUBLE AT THE HUTCH QUARTERS

It felt strange to Mitzy to be running alongside a dog she had heard so much about. Champ wasn't how Mitzy had imagined. He looked exactly as Biskit had described him but Mitzy had expected him to be friendlier somehow.

They ran behind Biskit as he crossed a road to avoid being spotted by the children in a school playground. Mitzy double-checked the road was clear. She knew that Biskit often forgot to use some of his other senses when he was tracking.

"So, Champ, it must be weird being back," said Mitzy.

"Back where?" Champ looked at her in confusion.

"On Earth?" said Mitzy.

"Oh, right. Yes… Really weird," said Champ.

Mitzy had always got the impression that Champ had been the sensible partner, compared to Biskit. But if that was the case, why had he broken his agency's rules and come back to Earth? Something didn't add up. She wanted to ask Biskit but he was too busy sniffing. He led them to a part of town with fewer shops and more houses.

"So you're the famous Champ," said Mitzy.

"What? Oh, right. Yes. I don't know how famous I am," he replied. "These Caboodle Brothers, they're *really* famous. Did you know they once stole two suns from the desert planet of Scorchio? They couldn't sell them, though. It turned out they were too hot."

"I've never heard of them," said Mitzy.

"Really? They've been to this planet before, too. It was before my time but I heard they caused a lot of trouble."

Biskit turned a corner and crouched down as they snuck past a shop with plastic bowls of fruit outside. Once they were clear of the shop, Champ joined her again and Mitzy saw that he was munching an apple.

"Hey, that's stealing," said Mitzy.

"We're hunting two of the greatest criminals the universe has ever known," said Champ. "I think these humans can afford one apple as payment."

The more she got to know Champ, the less she liked him. "You know, Biskit took it pretty badly when you disappeared like that," she said.

"It wasn't my fault. I was taken by the Snot Snatchers then recruited by the agency. I never had time to say goodbye."

Biskit led them past a young father trying to

persuade his daughter to get into her car seat.

"Biskit bumped into your owners recently," said Mitzy.

"How were they?" asked Champ.

"They'd moved on, bought a new dog."

"Good for them," said Champ.

Mitzy checked his eyes for any indication of sadness or regret. There was nothing. "Remind me what your owners were called again?" she said.

Champ turned and looked at her but then Biskit stopped suddenly. They were in a quiet street, across the road from a row of houses with neat lawns and colourful front doors. Parked outside one of the houses was the fizzy drinks lorry.

"That's the lorry I saw earlier," said Mitzy.

Biskit looked around. "This road is familiar," he said.

It took Mitzy a moment to recognize the

street. They usually approached from the alley behind the houses. "It's Commander F's house," she said.

"They're after the commander?" exclaimed Biskit.

"Maybe," said Champ. "We shouldn't rush into anything."

Biskit, Mitzy and Champ took cover behind a garden wall then poked their heads over to look at the lorry. The back doors were open, revealing vacuum-packed crates of cans stacked up inside.

"The Burp is in the house," said Biskit, his tail wagging excitedly. "We need to go in after it."

"Stick," said Champ. "His name is Stick and no, we shouldn't. We can't wander into a human house in the middle of the day to catch a creature that could be disguised as anything!"

"He's right," said Mitzy. "We need to stick to procedure. For all we know, the criminal we're after is a wasp flying through the house. Our priority is to keep Commander F safe."

"Unless the Burp's already got him," said Biskit.

"That's why we need to act now," said Mitzy. "You two, check out that lorry. I'll warn the grumpy bunny."

"She's a smart one, this new partner of yours." Champ winked at Biskit.

Mitzy eyed him suspiciously but she didn't have time to argue. "Biskit, watch him," she said before turning and bolting across the road towards the side passage of the house.

CHAPTER 9

SPONGY BUNNY BATH TIME

Mitzy found the gap under the fence into Commander F's back garden and wriggled through. She kept her head low as she padded around the flower beds. She could see movement inside the house. Commander F's owners were in – she would have to be careful. She snuck up to the hutch and heard Commander F making a strange noise. For a moment she thought he was speaking in some strange alien language ... then she realized he was singing.

"OOOoo-Luuuaaa-Goo-EEE..."

There was a strange bubbly sound to his voice, which Mitzy couldn't identify – then she saw that he was drinking from his water bottle and gurgling. His head was tipped back so he couldn't see her until she tapped on the cage. He instantly lowered his head and spat out a mouthful of water, spraying Mitzy in the face.

"Mitzy! What are you doing here?"

Mitzy wiped her face with a paw. "I've come to warn you about… Er, can I ask what you were doing, sir?"

"I was gargling! It's a bunny thing … it's not important. You can't just barge in here unannounced. Emily could come out at any moment."

"Yes, sir, but we have to get you to safety. You need to trust me."

"To safety? What are you talking about?"

"Please, sir," said Mitzy.

"Agent Mitzy," barked Commander F. "I am your commander-in-chief. If you know something, you have to tell me the whole story. What's going on? Is this something to do with communications being down?"

"Yes, that was Zed. He's a SUPA agent. So is Champ. He's here, too, but I'm not sure I trust him."

"Champ, Biskit's partner?"

"Yes, he works for the Special Universal Policing Agency," said Mitzy.

"Champ's a SUPA agent?"

"You know about the SUPA agency?"

"Of course I know," replied Commander F. "Now, what's going on?"

"Please, Commander, you have to come

with me at once. I'll explain everything once we've got you to safety. I was thinking the NERD lab would be a good place to hide out."

"Hide out?" exclaimed Commander F. "I'm not hiding from anything!"

The back door of the house opened so suddenly that Mitzy jumped. She dived behind the hutch as a young girl in dungarees stepped into the garden.

"It's Emily," whispered Commander F. "I am very disappointed in you, Agent Mitzy. By failing to follow procedure, you're endangering everything we stand for."

Emily approached the hutch and bent down, brushing her curly red hair from her face. "Oh, Fluffikins, there you are," she said. "Time for you to come and have a bath."

Mitzy could hear the scraping of Commander F's feet as he edged further into the hutch but he was unable to avoid Emily's grip. "I'll be back for you, Mitzy," he muttered as he was dragged out.

"Oh, Fluffikins, stop struggling," said Emily. "It's time for your spongy bunny bath, to make sure you don't get sticky poo-poos stuck on your bot-bot."

Mitzy caught a final glimpse of Commander F's furious face as he was carried off into the house.

Then Mitzy noticed something odd about Emily. She was walking with a limp. Emily wasn't Emily. She was Stick Caboodle, the Atomic Burp.

Mitzy broke her cover and ran after Commander F. The back door was closing but she slipped through just in time.

"Is that you, Emily?" she heard Emily's mother call.

"No, Mum," came a voice from upstairs. "I'm in my room."

"Your room? I thought I told you to get Fluffikins for his spongy bunny bath. You know how sticky his bot-bot gets."

Emily's mother stepped out of the kitchen just as Mitzy ran past. She screamed but Mitzy didn't even slow down – she was out of the door in a flash, following the fake Emily and Commander F out of the front door.

"Biskit! That's the Burp! It's got Commander F," yelled Mitzy.

The fake Emily threw Commander F into the back of the lorry and headed round the other side towards the driver's cab. Mitzy ran down the garden path and out on to the pavement. As she darted under the lorry, she

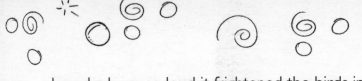

heard a burp so loud it frightened the birds in a nearby tree.

When Mitzy emerged from under the lorry, the Atomic Burp was back in his factory-worker disguise. "Stop right there," she yelled.

Stick Caboodle turned round.

"Biskit! Champ!" Mitzy shouted. "Where are you?"

She was expecting them to come bounding out to help but no one came.

"It looks like you're on your own," said the shapeshifter, climbing into the driver's cab.

As Mitzy ran to stop him, he kicked her away and slammed the door. She looked for something to latch on to but the lorry was already moving. He pulled out from the curb and she had to dive out of the way of one of the huge tyres. She landed in a rose bush and leaped up, only to find a thorn had got lodged in her paw. She tried to chase the lorry but it was too painful. By the time she had plucked the thorn out with her teeth, the lorry was at the end of the road.

"Biskit?" she yelled, frustrated and angry. "Champ? Where are you?"

An old lady pulling a shopping trolley stopped and bent down. "There there, puss. Are you lost? I've got some tasty treats at home, if you'd like."

Mitzy felt her stomach growl but there was no time for kindly old humans. She had to catch that lorry.

CHAPTER 10

•••

TWIST CABOODLE

Biskit jumped up into the back of the lorry, closely followed by Champ. Inside, crates of cans lined the sides, tied down to stop them rattling about when the vehicle was moving.

"Philip likes the strawberry lemonade one best," said Biskit. "I prefer the orange. What's the slogan? Drink Orange Zest to feel your best… Something like that."

"I couldn't say," said Champ.

"Champ, you've been away a long time but Sip Pop was around when you were here. Your owner Freddie used to let you have some when his parents weren't looking, didn't he?"

Champ didn't respond. He was tearing off the plastic cover and pulling out a can between his teeth.

"Are you all right, Champ?" asked Biskit. "What are you doing?"

Champ flicked open the ring pull with his teeth and tipped his head back to guzzle down the contents.

"Er, Champ?" said Biskit.

"No," said Champ,

"What?"

"I'm not Champ," said Champ. "You knew it really. I don't smell like Champ, I don't behave like Champ and your old goody-two-shoes partner would never break the rules by returning to his home planet."

"*You're* one of them." Biskit's astonishment gave way to anger. He had known something was wrong. He should have trusted his instincts. But he had wanted to believe that his partner was back.

Champ let out an enormous burp that had a sickly sweet smell of fresh apples. His skin rippled and his furry coat slid away to reveal a spiky blue alien.

"The name is Twist Caboodle," he said.

The alien lurched forwards and grabbed Biskit's collar. Biskit fought to get free. He would have succeeded had Twist not let out another transforming burp that turned him into an enormous spider with a lion's mane. He fired out sticky webbing that wrapped itself tightly around Biskit.

"Sorry, Biskit," said Twist. "You may be a big deal in this town but you're no match for one of the greatest intergalactic robbers the universe has ever known."

"I don't understand. You were the one who came to find *me*!" said Biskit.

Twist downed another can then let out a burp that smelled of cranberry and gone-off milk, which returned him to his natural spiky blue self.

"You want me to fill you in, do you?" said Twist. "Oh, all right. Stick escaped the prison

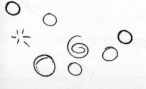

cell before me. I knew he'd come to Earth
but I needed a way of tracking him down. So
when I got out I borrowed the identity of the
SUPA agent who arrested us. I hid onboard
his partner's ship and came to find you. Then
all I had to do was lend you the SUPA Super
Smeller to find Stick."

Twist knocked the gadget off Biskit's nose.
Biskit tried to stop him but he was bound too
tightly.

"I knew you'd find him if your sense of smell
was as good as Champ said. And my plan
worked perfectly," said Twist. He dropped
the SUPA Super Smeller and stamped on it,
sending sparks flying and destroying the device
in an instant.

"But how did you even know about me?"
asked Biskit.

"My brother and I spent a long time on
Champ's ship after he caught us. Our scent

may not have rubbed off on *him* but he had quite an effect on us. Your old partner talks about you and your pathetic little planet all the time."

"Why are you here if you think it's pathetic?" demanded Biskit.

"Why do thieves go anywhere?" said Twist. "To steal things."

The lorry door opened and Commander F was thrown inside. The bunny slammed into a crate of fizzy drinks, causing one to fall and land on Biskit's head.

"Ow," yelped Biskit.

"What's going on?" demanded Commander F. "Biskit, what's happening?"

"Get out, sir," said Biskit.

Commander F turned round but the door slammed shut.

Twist let out another burp and transformed into a large purple three-headed slug. He

coughed up a mouthful of disgusting yellow goo, which landed on Commander F and quickly solidified, pinning him to the bottom of the lorry.

"That's Solidified Slug Slime from the Sargoonian Sand Slug of the Sulwork Solar System," said Twist.

"The Atomic Burp Brothers, I presume," snarled Commander F.

Twist burped himself back to his natural form. "Indeed. We've returned."

The crates of cans rattled as the lorry began to move. Another one dropped on Biskit's head. "Ow. What do you mean returned?"

"They came here before," said Commander F. "It was before your time. Old Mo was on that job. Now, *there* was a good agent. Quick, smart, not tied up in the back of a lorry."

Biskit ignored Commander F's dig at him.

"Yes, I recognized him when I saw him at the kennels," said Twist. "It's a good thing he's lost his sense of smell. He was the one who sniffed us out the last time."

"What were you stealing then?" asked Biskit.

"Forget-Me-Plop," said Commander F. "That's what they were after then and that's what they're after now. I imagine the ability to make people forget is pretty useful stuff for a couple of common thieves."

"You'll find out how common we are when

we get what we want." Twist bowed down and pushed a spiky finger into Commander F's chin.

Biskit tried to wriggle free of the sticky webbing that bound his limbs together. On the other side of the lorry, Commander F was getting nowhere with the solid slug slime. Twist turned a stalk eye to look at Biskit and said, "You can struggle all you like. We once used that webbing to tie up the whole staff of the Pan Dimensional Gold Vaults of Trumple-Donling."

"Release me at once, you overgrown blue cactus," yelled Commander F.

"If you don't like me like this, maybe I should change." Twist gulped down a can and with a **BU**u**u**u**u**u**UU**u**URRP!** turned into an exact copy of Commander F.

"Who's that supposed to be?" demanded Commander F.

"Er…" Biskit hesitated. "It's you, sir."

"Me? Look at the size of him. He's much too big," said Commander F.

Twist laughed. "Yes, you've put on a few pounds since we last met."

"You'll be sorry, you sniffling shapeshifter," said Commander F. "You won't get away with this. You'll be locked up again soon enough."

"Locked up? The Caboodle Brothers never remain behind bars for long. That's the thing about Atomic Burps, we're better out than in."

CHAPTER 11

*

ZED GETS ZAPPED!

Mitzy stopped suddenly at the side of the road. A car beeped as it zoomed past, blocking her way and allowing the fizzy drinks lorry to escape. She knew Biskit would have made it across the road. He would never have let fear for his own life get in the way of pursuing a threat. She had failed to save Commander F.

"Ah, Agent Mitzy, excellent news, everything's up and working again now," squeaked a voice behind her.

Mitzy turned around to find a seagull

standing on a postbox. Example One's voice
was coming through a speaker attached to the
bird's leg.

"Example One," said Mitzy. "Am I glad to
hear your voice!"

"I don't know. Are you glad?" asked
Example One.

The seagull pecked
the top of the postbox.

"It's the Atomic
Burps," exclaimed
Mitzy. "They've taken
Commander F."

"The Atomic Burps have returned?" said Example One. "Oh dear, I imagine they were a bit upset after the last time they came here."

"Why? What happened?" asked Mitzy.

"It was Agent Mo's idea. Now, there was an agent with brains. We allowed the Burps to make off with a barrel-load of what they thought was Forget-Me-Plop. Except it wasn't that at all. They left with five gallons of bird droppings."

Mitzy knew Biskit would have laughed at this but he wasn't there and she was in no mood for bird-poo jokes.

"We need to find out where they're going," she said urgently.

"I know exactly where they'll be going. They'll be heading here. They're after our supplies again," said Example One.

"OK, I'm on my way," said Mitzy. "Don't let

anyone in."

"Yes, good idea," said
Example One.

The seagull flew off and
Mitzy was about to spring into
action when a door slid open in the postbox
and Zed appeared. "Need a lift?" he said,
slinking out of his spaceship.

"How did you get there?" asked Mitzy. "And
how did you find me?"

"I'm monitoring your whole network," said
Zed. "You're not that hard to find."

"Why did it take so long to get the system
back online?" asked Mitzy.

"Someone messed with my control panel,"
said Zed.

"Champ," said Mitzy. "I'll bet it was Champ.
He's working with them."

"He *is* them … or rather *one* of them,"
said Zed. "He's got your partner. Come on. I'll

show you how the big cats do business."

He swished his tail around as he strolled back into the ship. Mitzy followed him in and tried not to look too impressed with the gleaming interior. Zed jumped up on the counter and hit a few buttons. The door closed and the ship made a whirring, spinning sound.

"It looks like it's down to the cats to save the dogs as usual," said Zed.

"How long will it take to get there?" asked Mitzy.

"We're already here," replied Zed.

Zed pushed a button and the door slid open. They were no longer outside Commander F's house but had arrived by the Pet Defenders' secret lab. Mitzy stepped out and turned around to see that the spaceship was now disguised as a yellow skip.

"This ship is amazing!" she asked. "How does it work?"

"Very well, thank you," replied Zed. "Take cover… They're coming."

Mitzy and Zed dived under an abandoned car as the fizzy drinks lorry turned off the road and came to a standstill. The green spiky driver

jumped out, and limped around to the back of the lorry. He opened the door and reappeared clutching a large angry white rabbit, wriggling and trying to get free.

"He's got Commander F," said Mitzy.

"Wait," said Zed. "We don't know if that's the commander or Twist in disguise. The one carrying him is definitely Stick. I recognize the limp."

"But what if it is the *real*
commander?" asked Mitzy.

"I'm not rushing into anything," said Zed. "I need to see what they want."

"No," said Mitzy. "We need to defend our planet. If you won't get him, I will." She curled her tail round Zed's, took aim with his tail gun then stuck her nose under his chin and nudged the blue button on his collar.

The laser beam fired out and struck Stick, instantly freezing him. The rabbit jumped out of his arms and ran towards the lab. Mitzy looked up at the seagulls standing on the building and hovering above. She knew Example One would be watching the whole thing on the cameras.

"Open up and let me in," barked the rabbit. "Can't you see I'm under attack?"

Mitzy darted out into the open. "Commander F. It's me, Mitzy."

The rabbit looked at her for a moment then banged on the door again. "The Atomic Burp is disguised as Agent Mitzy. Launch a Forget-Me-Plop attack immediately."

"Oh, great work," said Zed, emerging from under the lorry. "Sorry, Mitzy, this is nothing personal but I have a job to do."

He pointed his tail gun at her and pushed the blue button. The light at the end flashed. Mitzy had no time to lose. She spun around, flicking her tail so that it wrapped round his. Before Zed knew what was happening, Mitzy had shifted his aim so that the blue beam missed her by a whisker and hit the black cat instead.

Zed froze.

"It's always personal," said Mitzy. "Now, if you don't mind, I have a job to do, too."

CHAPTER 12

A LOST EXAMPLE

Commander F was rarely the happiest bunny in the world, but Biskit had never seen him as furious as when he was struggling to free himself from the yellow slime.

"Agent Biskit," growled the commander, "you walking bag of fleas, I'm holding you responsible for this. You're supposed to be one of my top agents and yet here we are tied up in the back of a lorry, while an alien disguised as me is walking into our secret lab and causing who-knows-what sort of havoc? Never mind suspension, when I get out of this,

I'm going to ex—"

"Exclaim your extreme gratitude?" Biskit offered. He was standing in front of the furious rabbit, no longer bound by the webbing.

"You're free!" said Commander F.

"Of course. Give me long enough and I can bite through anything. Would you like me to help free you or was there something you were going to say?"

"Harrumph," muttered Commander F.

Biskit sank his teeth into the crusted slime covering.

"Ow. Watch where you're putting those canines."

With his back to the door, Biskit didn't notice it get nudged open until he heard Mitzy's voice say, "You two look cosy."

He turned around to see his partner standing in the doorway. "Mitzy," he said.

Commander F shook himself free from the

slime shell. "Oh, nice try," he said. "Fool me once, shame on you. Fool me twice, shame on *me*."

"What?" said Mitzy.

"You're one of them!" He pounced forwards with his paws outstretched, slamming into Mitzy and sending both of them flying out of the back of the lorry. Mitzy tried to escape but Commander F landed on her with a **FLUH-DUMP!**

"Ow," she cried, reluctant to fight back against her boss.

He pushed a paw into her cheek and in a low, threatening growl said, "Which one are you? Stick or Twist?"

"Er, sir," said Biskit, hopping out of the lorry.

"What is it?" snapped Commander F. "I'm

doing your job for you here. Now, help me tie
up this crook."

"As entertaining as this is," said Biskit, "that's
not the Atomic Burp."

"Says who?"

"My nose, sir," said Biskit. "That's Mitzy."

"Are you sure?" said Commander F.

"Yes."

"Oh." He climbed off Mitzy and she stood
up straight.

"Don't go demanding an apology," said
Commander F.

"It doesn't matter, sir," said Mitzy. "Come on."

Biskit, Mitzy and Commander F ran around
the side of the lorry where they could see the
lab door. There was no sign of either of the
Caboodle Brothers but Zed was still standing
frozen to the spot.

"Who's that?" asked Commander F.

"SUPA agent Zed. Where's everyone else?"

asked Mitzy.

"Er, I think they may be taking cover," said Biskit. "Look." A squadron of seagulls swooped down towards them.

"Under the lorry," yelled Mitzy.

"I will not hide from my own gulls," replied Commander F.

"Yes, but they're following the orders of a different you," said Biskit.

Biskit and Mitzy dived under the lorry but Commander F stood waving his paws furiously at the birds.

"A different me?" he yelled. "Nonsense. I'm Commander F and my seagulls would never launch an attack on m—"

The seagulls dropped their loads of Forget-Me-Plop, showering the rabbit with white gunk and instantly wiping all thoughts from Commander F's mind. "Er, what was I saying?"

"Who cares?" Twist Caboodle stepped out of the lab. "I ordered the attack. I was you then, whereas now I am me."

"Who are you?" demanded Commander F. "Now I think about it, who am I?"

"You are unimportant," said Stick, joining his brother.

Both were in their natural form.

"Unlike your friend here." Twist raised his hand, revealing that he had Example One clutched tightly in his fist.

"Let me go, you villain," said Example One.

"Why would I do that?" asked Twist. "You're the reason my brother and I came back to this silly planet. You tricked us last time with that fake Forget-Me-Plop. Next time we need it, you will make it exactly as we want it."

"And not just that," said Stick. "You will work for us, making inventions that will stop us ever being caught again."

"I'll never help you crooks," said Example One.

"Of course you will," said Stick. "You'll have no other choice."

Biskit and Mitzy stepped out from the lorry, avoiding the puddles of Forget-Me-Plop and keeping a careful eye on the seagulls that were perched on the rooftop, awaiting instructions.

"This is the end for you," said Mitzy. "Put down the mouse and raise your hands."

Twist and Stick laughed.

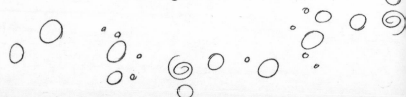

"One more step and I'll crush him," said Twist.

Stick grinned. "Yes, we're calling the shots now. You're going to tell us what Zed's ship is disguised as, then you're going to watch us fly away. You'll do this because you know that if you try to stop us, you can kiss goodbye to your mouse friend."

Twist tightened his grip on Example One.

"Ow, stop squeezing me!" said the pink mouse. "You've snapped my stylus."

"Stop," said Mitzy. "It's the skip. The ship is the skip."

"Thank you," said Stick. "Now, be good little pets and sit."

"Yes. Stay," said Twist.

Mitzy and Biskit watched helplessly as the Caboodle Brothers reached Zed's ship. Stick downed a can, burped and transformed into Zed. While the real Zed remained rooted to the spot, covered in Forget-Me-Plop, his doppelganger pressed a paw to the skip and a door slid open

"See you around, Pet Defenders." Stick limped inside.

"I'm afraid we've won this time," said Twist.

"Oh, this is not good," said Example One. "Not good at—"

His final words were lost behind the hiss of the sliding door. Biskit and Mitzy darted forwards but it was too late. After a moment of whirring and shimmering, the skip vanished.

"Where's it gone?" asked Biskit.

"It could be anywhere," said Mitzy. "We've lost them. We've lost Example One. We've failed."

CHAPTER 13

🐾

THE UNMISTAKER

If there had been any human witnesses there that day, they would have been faced with the unusual scene of a confused rabbit covered in goo, a frozen black cat with a flashing collar and a dog running round in circles, barking at a tabby cat.

"We need to go after them," said Biskit.

"Where?" said Mitzy. "They're in a ship capable of slipping through the molecules of the universe. We have no way of following them, no way of catching them and no way of saving Example One. We're out of options."

"What are you two talking about?" asked Commander F. "What just happened? The last thing I remember I was at home, practising my garg— It doesn't matter. I wasn't *here*."

"A pair of Atomic Burps just walked off our planet with Example One," said Mitzy.

"The Burps are back? That sounds bad," said Commander F. "So, who messed up?"

"It was my fault," said Mitzy, lowering her head. "I should have worked with Zed, not turned his own Stare Ray on him."

"Stare Ray? Zed?" said Commander F, noticing the frozen cat. "What the crusty carrot is wrong with this cat?"

"No, I'm to blame," said Biskit. "A good agent trusts his nose. I knew there was something funny about Champ. I wanted so much for it to be him."

"What are you even doing here? Didn't I suspend you?" Commander F twitched his nose angrily at Biskit.

Mitzy licked her paw and said, "Biskit, anyone would have made the same mistake... Hold on, that's it." Her eyes widened.

"What's what?" barked Commander F.

"We've made a mistake," said Mitzy, waving her tail excitedly.

"Great. Er, but how does that help us?" asked Biskit.

"We can undo it!"

"What are you meowing about?" demanded Commander F.

"The *Unmistaker*," said Mitzy. "Biskit, I'll need your help." She ran over to Zed and adjusted his tail gun so that it was pointing at the spot where the disguised spaceship had been.

"Which colour does what?" asked Biskit, peering at Zed's collar.

"Red's a blaster, blue is a stare gun. We want the green, the unmistaker," said Mitzy.

"What will it do?"

"It doesn't do. It undoes."

"Undoes what?"

"Mistakes," said Mitzy. "Hit the button!"

Biskit pressed it and a green laser beam fired out of the gun, creating ripples in the air.

"Keep it held down," he heard Mitzy say.

Slowly but surely, the yellow skip reappeared. Then the door opened and Twist Caboodle walked backwards out of the ship, still clutching Example One. His brother was next, still in the form of Zed and also walking backwards.

"When I say so, press the red button," said Mitzy.

To Biskit's surprise the green laser was transporting the ship and the Burps back to the point just before they stepped on to the ship.

When Mitzy yelled, "Now!" Biskit switched to the red button and the laser changed colour. There was a high-pitched sound, followed by a low rumbling then an enormous bang as the deadly ray blasted a hole in the ship.

The force of the explosion sent everyone flying backwards. Biskit and Mitzy rolled over then leaped to their feet, while Zed went flying into Commander F.

The explosion must have damaged the ship's camouflage setting because, as the smoke cleared, it no longer looked like a skip. It looked like an extremely shiny if somewhat broken spacecraft. Beside it lay a pair of spiky, and rather dazed, Atomic Burps. Example One slipped out from between Twist's fingers.

"Example One, run for it," cried Biskit.

The mouse didn't argue. He scurried back into the secret lab.

"Let's get them," said Mitzy.

"Yeah, we'll teach them to take our mouse," said Biskit.

But Twist and Stick were back on their feet and already reaching for a can of pop each. Two disgusting burps later, they reappeared except they had transformed into a scruffy mongrel and a tabby cat.

CHAPTER 14

LET'S GET US

"Let's get them," said Biskit.

"Except they're us," said Mitzy.

"Then let's get us!" said Biskit.

The seagulls perched on the
rooftop, capturing everything
on their leg cameras as Biskit and Mitzy
approached the identical copies
of themselves.

"I'll take me, you take you," said Biskit.

"Sounds good to me," replied Mitzy. Having
once fought Biskit while he was under the
control of an alien beard, she had no desire
to repeat the experience.

Approaching the disguised Atomic Burp,

she felt as though she was walking towards her own reflection, except that the cat she was facing walked with a limp and wore an evil smile.

"It's just you and me now," said Stick. "Or rather, it's just you and you."

"You think you're so smart," said Mitzy, "but we stopped you escaping."

"We'll find another way off this planet," said Stick. "In the end the Caboodle Brothers always get what they want."

Mitzy extended her claws and tensed her muscles, ready to pounce. Stick did the same. Both their whiskers bristled and then they jumped. There was a **MEOW-SCREOW-YATCH** as the pair of identical cats collided. Mitzy swiped at Stick's back. He scraped her belly. She kicked his right leg so that his weight fell on his weaker left leg. He staggered. Mitzy sunk her teeth

into the loose bit of skin around Stick's neck.
He kicked her off but she managed to land on
her feet with a mouthful of her own fur.

She spun around to see Stick guzzling
down a can. He gave a burp and began
transforming into a lizard-like creature with
rough scaly skin and a head that kept growing
and growing.

"Move," said a voice.

She turned around to see Zed with his tail
gun pointing at her.

"I said move."

Mitzy stepped to the side so the gun was
pointing at Stick. Zed's chin was poised over
the purple button. Mitzy took another couple
of steps back and Zed fired. The beam shot
out and hit Stick right in the chest. Whatever
he was trying to turn into, he was still changing
when the laser hit him. He dropped to the
floor, half-cat, half-lizard.

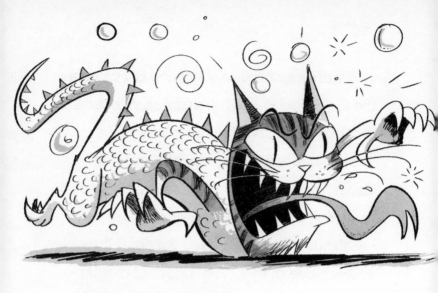

"YAAAARGH," screamed Stick.

"What have you done to me?"

"Discombobulater," said Zed. "Your atoms don't know what to do. You're neither one thing or another."

"Nice gadget," said Mitzy.

"Sorry? Do I know you?" said Zed.

Mitzy realized that Zed was still dripping with Forget-Me-Plop.

"How much do you remember?" she asked him.

"I remember arriving here. I was looking for the Caboodle Brothers," said Zed. "Looks like I've found one of them."

Stick was writhing on the ground, desperately trying to let out a burp big enough to complete his transformation.

"Where's the other one?" asked Zed.

"He's one of those two dogs," said Mitzy.

When they turned to see how Biskit was getting on with Twist, it was impossible to distinguish one dog from the other. The identical mongrels were spinning round and round, biting and scratching as they fought.

"Biskit!" yelled Mitzy.

"Yes, that's me," replied both dogs. "No, it's me not him… Get that one."

"I tell you what," said Zed, "I'll blast them both to be sure."

"No," said Mitzy. "Give Biskit a chance."

"I can't take any more risks," said Zed.

The dogs were rolling on the ground, fighting tooth and nail. One jumped on to the other's back only to be thrown off instantly. They snarled and growled at each other.

"Mitzy, give me a hand here, will you?" said one of the Biskits, turning to look at her.

"Of course," replied Mitzy.

But she didn't move. Instead she whispered to Zed, "That one. Shoot that one."

"You think that's the Burp?" said Zed.

"I'm sure of it," she replied.

"Let's find out if you're right." Zed fired the purple beam, but his target dodged out of the way and the beam hit the lorry, blasting a hole in the side and releasing a mountain of drinks cans that tumbled to the ground.

The Biskit who had asked for help jumped up and grabbed a can in his mouth, clicking it open with his claws and downing the liquid.

"Now!" yelled Mitzy.

Zed fired.

The Atomic Burp was trying to turn into some kind of flying insect. His wings were unfurling but he still had Biskit's head as he dropped to the ground.

The real Biskit stood up and brushed himself down. "Thanks," he said. "How did you know that was Twist?"

"Because he asked for help," said Mitzy.

"Good work, both of you," said Zed. "Now, where's my ship?"

CHAPTER 15

MOVE ON AND MOVE IN

SUPA agent Zed was not overjoyed about the state of his ship but when Mitzy explained what had happened, he accepted it. Example One and his mice offered to help repair it, while the Pet Defenders ensured that Stick and Twist Caboodle were secured in one of the ship's prison cells.

Commander F grabbed them as they stepped out of the ship. "My memory is a bit fuzzy," he said, "but I'll be watching all this back on the seagull network and letting you know where you went wrong. Now, I'd better go and find some seagulls to help deal with my Emily and her parents. I'm not happy about having to wipe the memories of my owners. Not happy at all."

The Pet Defenders didn't reply. Neither of them was used to seeing their commander so confused or so upset. Zed joined them as Commander F hopped off to find some seagulls.

"That's it, small worlders protecting your owners from the truth," said Zed. "I mean, these humans, are you sure they couldn't cope with knowing?"

"They have enough problems here on Earth without learning of all the dangers out in the universe," said Biskit.

"It's your decision," said Zed, "but in my experience, there aren't many secrets that stay secret forever. Speaking of which, there are some parts of the ship I'd rather your mice didn't touch. They're not bad workers though – and Example One knows his stuff. I think I may have underestimated your agency."

"You wouldn't be the first," said Mitzy.

"Well, if you ever want to work for a *real* agency, I can put in a recommendation," said Zed.

"Thanks but I'm an Earth cat," said Mitzy.

Zed turned to Biskit. "What about you? I know Champ would love to see you again."

"He knows where I am," said Biskit. "Right here on Earth, doing my job."

Zed smiled. "Fair enough. Now, I'd better go and check on those mice."

Zed disappeared into the ship, leaving Biskit and Mitzy alone.

"Speaking of home," said Biskit, "I suppose I'd better get back to the kennels before Mrs Stroganov calls Philip and ruins his holiday."

"How is it there?" asked Mitzy.

"It could be worse," said Biskit. "Besides, Philip deserves a break."

"You're a good pet, Biskit," said Mitzy.

"You, too," he replied.

"I don't have an owner," said Mitzy sadly. "Remember?"

Biskit took a couple of steps away then turned around and walked back. "Mitzy," he said, "I think you should move in with me and Philip. Once he's back, I mean."

"Move in?" said Mitzy. "But isn't Philip a dog person?"

"He's a pet person," said Biskit. "He'll look after you, I know he will. You'll have somewhere to sleep and a food bowl that's never empty."

"I … I don't know what to say, Biskit."

"Say yes," said Biskit.

"Thank you," Mitzy replied, trying to hide the tear in her eye.

"It shouldn't have taken this long to ask," said Biskit. "Pets look after each other."

Unsure what to say, they looked over at Commander F, who was shouting at one of the seagulls, "When you drop the Forget-Me-Plop on my Emmsy-wemsy, do it as gently as possible. Remember, she's only a child."

"Do you think he's forgotten he suspended you?" asked Mitzy.

"I'm not going to hang around to find out," said Biskit.

"I'll come with you. I don't think he's best pleased with me either after I barged into his garden like that," said Mitzy.

Biskit and Mitzy hopped on to a small crumbly brick wall and looked up at the crescent moon.

"It's funny," said Biskit. "Both me and Champ ending up with cat partners."

"Do you think you'll ever see him for real?" said Mitzy.

"Who knows?" said Biskit. "It's good to know he's all right."

Mitzy laughed.

"What's so funny?" asked Biskit.

"I just remembered something I wanted to tell you. What do you want to hear about first? The gargling practice or the spongy bunny bath time?"

"I can still hear you," yelled Commander F. "Agent Mitzy, don't you dare!"

But the Pet Defenders were already leaping off the wall, vanishing into the alleyways of Nothington-on-Sea, ready to protect those who protected them.